... Imitate those who through faith and patience inherit what has been promised.

—Hebrews 6:12

ZONDERKIDZ

The Berenstain Bears® Reap the Harvest
Previously published by Reader's Digest Kids as *The Berenstain Bears and the Summer Job*
Copyright © 1994, 2011 by Berenstain Publishing, Inc.
Illustrations © 1994, 2011 by Berenstain Publishing, Inc.

Requests for information should be addressed to:

Zonderkidz, Grand Rapids, Michigan 49530

Library of Congress Cataloging-in-Publication Data

Berenstain, Stan, 1923–2005.
    [Berenstain Bears and the summer job]
    The Berenstain Bears reap the harvest / created by Stan & Jan Berenstain with
Mike Berenstain.
      p. cm.
    ISBN 978-0-310-72277-9 (hardcover, printed)
    [1. Summer employment—Fiction. 2. Farm life—Fiction. 3. Christian life—Fiction.
4. Brothers and sisters—Fiction. 5. Bears—Fiction.] I. Berenstain, Jan, 1923-. II.
Berenstain, Mike, 1951- III. Title.
    PZ7.B4483Bfef 2011
  [E]—dc22   2010031942

Editor: Mary Hassinger
Art direction: Cindy Davis

Printed in China

11 12 13 14 15 16 /SCC/ 10 9 8 7 6 5 4 3 2

The Berenstain Bears.

REAP
THE
HARVEST

by Stan and Jan Berenstain
with Mike Berenstain

ZONDERVAN.com/
AUTHORTRACKER
follow your favorite authors

ZONDERkidz

Living
Lights™

Beginning Reader

It was summertime. School was closed for the year. Brother and Sister Bear were walking down a dusty road. They were thinking about how they should spend their summer vacation.

"We could just play," said Sister.

"Playing is fine," said Brother. "But playing all the time would be boring."

"We could go swimming," said Sister.

"Swimming is fine," said Brother.
"But we can't go swimming every day."

"We could go to the library," said Sister.

"Yes," said Brother. "Mama takes us to the library every Saturday. But what will we do the rest of the week?"

"Maybe we could get a job!" said Sister. "Papa says according to Proverbs, 'All hard work brings a profit.' Maybe we can make some money."

"That's a good idea," said Brother. "But what kind of job could we get? We're just cubs."

That's when they saw the sign. It was
hanging on Farmer Ben's front gate. It said:
HELP WANTED. SEE FARMER BEN.

"Well, yes," said Farmer Ben. "I do need help. But I was thinking of someone older. What could you cubs do to help?"

"All kinds of things," said the cubs.

"We could sweep the barn,

feed the chickens,

collect the eggs,

"Hmmm," said Farmer Ben. He thought for a while. Then he said, "All right. The job is yours. Here are some brooms. You can start by sweeping the barn."

"There's just one thing," said Sister. "If this is a job, we should get paid."

"Yes," said Brother. "How much will you pay us?"

"Hmmm," said Ben. "See that field? That's
my cornfield, and corn is my cash crop."

"What's a cash crop?" asked Sister.

"A cash crop is what a farmer grows to make money," said Brother.

"I'll tell you what," said Ben. He took a piece of string and some sticks and marked off a corner of the field.

"If you do a good job, I'll pay you the money I get for all the corn that grows in that corner of the field."

"How much will that be?" asked Sister.

"Depends," said Farmer Ben.

"Depends on what?" asked Brother.

"Depends on how much rain the Good Lord sends our way," said Ben. "Not too little; not too much. Depends on cornbugs. In a bad year, cornbugs can ruin a crop. Depends on keeping the crows from eating the seed—

that's why I'm making this scarecrow."

"So we won't know how much money we'll earn until the end of the summer," said Sister.

"No more than I will," said Farmer Ben. "That's the way it is with farming. Same way it is with faith … our true reward comes later on—in God's good time."

So the cubs went to work.

They swept the barn.

They fed
the chickens.

They collected the eggs.

They slopped the hogs.

They called the cows.

HERE BOSSIE

They made sure the bull pen was locked tight.

And they kept a close watch on their corner of the cornfield!

Brother watched the sky for rain.

Sister had bad dreams about cornbugs.

And when the crows were no longer afraid of Farmer Ben's scarecrow, Brother and Sister made a scarier one. It even scared Farmer Ben.

Working on the farm was hard, but it was fun too.

Brother and Sister both loved and respected all of God's creatures. And they made friends with the animals—

the chickens,

the pigs,

the cows.

Even Ben's big bull seemed
to like Brother and Sister.

But the best thing was having their own corner of the cornfield. The corn grew straight and tall and healthy.

"Farmer Ben told me the book of Timothy says, 'The hardworking farmer should be the first to receive a share of the crops,'" quoted Brother.

"Yessir," said Ben as he
got ready to harvest the corn.
"This is the finest cash crop
I've grown in years. You cubs
are going to do all right."

And they did. Their corner of the cornfield earned them many, many dollars. The farm had been blessed with a fine harvest indeed.

"Well," said Farmer Ben as he paid the cubs, "you should be proud of the good job you did all summer. Now don't spend it all in one place."

"We won't," said Brother. "But we will *put* it all in one place—the bank!"

"That's right," said Sister. "It took us a long time to earn this money. We want to keep it at least as long as it took to earn it."